my tooth
ith loothe

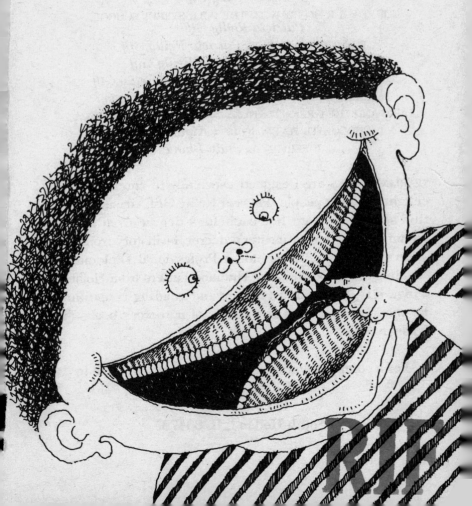

OTHER YEARLING BOOKS YOU WILL ENJOY:

THE SPOOK MATINEE AND OTHER SCARY POEMS FOR KIDS,
George Ulrich

WRITE UP A STORM WITH THE POLK STREET SCHOOL,
Patricia Reilly Giff

COUNT YOUR MONEY WITH THE POLK STREET SCHOOL,
Patricia Reilly Giff

THE POSTCARD PEST, *Patricia Reilly Giff*

TURKEY TROUBLE, *Patricia Reilly Giff*

LOOK OUT, WASHINGTON, D.C.!, *Patricia Reilly Giff*

AMOS'S KILLER CONCERT CAPER, *Gary Paulsen*

DUNC AND THE GREASED STICKS OF DOOM, *Gary Paulsen*

CHOCOLATE FEVER, *Robert Kimmel Smith*

SUPERFUDGE, *Judy Blume*

YEARLING BOOKS are designed especially to entertain and enlighten young people. Patricia Reilly Giff, consultant to this series, received her bachelor's degree from Marymount College and a master's degree in history from St. John's University. She holds a Professional Diploma in Reading and a Doctorate of Humane Letters from Hofstra University. She was a teacher and reading consultant for many years, and is the author of numerous books for young readers.

For a complete listing of all Yearling titles, write to
Dell Readers Service,
P.O. Box 1045,
South Holland, IL 60473.

my tooth ith loothe

Funny Poems to Read Instead of Doing Your Homework

WRITTEN AND ILLUSTRATED BY
GEORGE ULRICH

A Yearling Book

for Josh and Matt

Published by
Bantam Doubleday Dell Books for Young Readers
a division of
Bantam Doubleday Dell Publishing Group, Inc.
1540 Broadway
New York, New York 10036

The trademarks Yearling® and Dell® are registered in the
U.S. Patent and Trademark Office and in other countries.

ISBN: 0-440-41143-2

Printed in the United States of America
September 1995
10   9   8   7   6   5   4

CONTENTS

MY TOOTH ITH LOOTHE

My tooth ith loothe! My toothe ith loothe!
I can't go to thchool, that'th my excuthe.
It wath fine latht night when I went to bed,
But today it'th hanging by a thread!

My tooth ith loothe! My tooth ith loothe!
I'm telling you the honetht truth.
It maketh me want to jump and thout!
My tooth ith loothe. . . . Oopth! Now it'th out!

6

LAZY HEAD

Because I slept till half past eight,
I might be just a little late.
It's really not a federal crime
Not to get to school on time!

Okay! Okay! Okay! Okay!
So I didn't brush my teeth today.
And please don't shout, break into tears,
'cause I didn't wash behind my ears!

It's no big deal; don't be irate,
It's not the first time I've been late.
Since I missed the bus, as you just said,
I might as well go back to bed!

THE MEAN OLD MAN

One day I met a mean old man,
Turned out he was a wizard.
He changed my dog into a frog
And me into a lizard.

We had to move out of the house,
Into this slimy bog.
Eating bugs and crawly things
With other lizards, toads, and frogs.

I'm really glad he did it, though.
I really think it's cool.
'cause now we live beneath this rock
And never go to school!

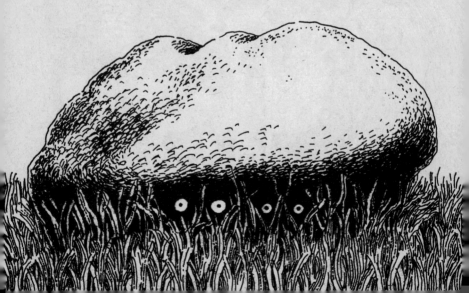

ALIEN EXCUSE

Dear Mrs. Brown,

Please excuse
Freddy's absence yesterday.
It seems an alien spaceship
Shot him with a ray.

He turned into a monster,
With three heads and fifteen eyes,
Orange hair, purple ears—
It caught me by surprise!

I took him to the doctor's,
Fed him soup and tea.
By suppertime he seemed to be
Behaving normally.

So Mrs. Brown, that is why
The test you gave the others,
Little Freddy had to miss.

Sincerely,
Freddy's Mother

MY BEST REPORT CARD EVER

No, I don't have my report card,
And in case you're wondering why,
It was stolen by some aliens
That came down from the sky!

There must have been a hundred!
They landed in the yard.
They aimed their ray guns at me
And stole my report card!

I wanted you to see it!
(I think I had straight A's.)
But when I tried to grab it back,
They zapped me with their rays!

When I came to my senses,
They were gone and I was sad,
They'd taken the best report card
That I had ever had!

ZACK AND ZEE

In our school
There was a rule
To line up alphabetically.
Which wasn't bad
Unless you had
A name that began with Z.

Poor Yolanda Zack
Was always in back
Of every line, you see.
She was always the last
When into our class
Came a kid named Zelda Zee!

Now when all of us
Wait for the bus,
Yolanda feels just fine!
With a grin and a smile
Like a crocodile,
No longer the last in line!

BURP!

Breakfast is my favorite meal.
I eat three grapefruit with the peel.
Then a dozen eggs Mom fries,
A bowl of oatmeal, two apple pies.

I grab my coat and a paper sack,
Three sandwiches for my morning snack;
Two apples and some chips to munch,
Just to tide me over until lunch!

After school I eat ten Oreos
Heat up three cans of SpaghettiOs
(As an afternoon pick-me-upper)
Then I sit at the table and wait for supper!

WORMS

Worms are juicy!
Worms are neat!
Worms are really good to eat!

I like 'em boiled,
I like 'em fried,
I like 'em every way I've tried!

So when I'm hungry
And my tummy churns,
I open up a can of worms!

DROOL AT SCHOOL

Out of the sewer the *thing* appeared.
All other creatures shrank back in fear.
It had slimy skin, dripped yellow drool,
And made a beeline for our school!

It crept into the kitchen; I sneaked a look.
It put on an apron and started to cook.
Worms and frogs, slugs by the bunch,
Went into the stew they'd be serving for lunch.

It's no surprise to kids who eat there.
Who come in at noon and take their seats there.
The stuff they're served is gross and crude;
It's what they call Cafeteria Food!

GUTS FOR LUNCH?

On Monday they serve gopher guts
And fingernail soufflé.
Tuesday we get chicken heads
And pizza made of clay.
Wednesday it's always sloppy joes
Made from flies and bugs.
On Thursday it's spaghetti
That's really worms and slugs.
Friday's always special,
Fried snakes in fish-eye glue,
That's why I bring my lunch from home,
You'd be smart if you did too!

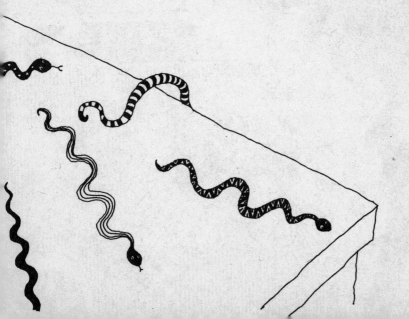

CHOPPED-LIVER BLUES

It's lunchtime at last! Hooray! Hooray!
Let's see what Mom put in my lunch today;
A chopped-liver sandwich with limburger spread,
Two slices of onion on thick garlic bread.

So why do I sit here alone in my seat?
And why doesn't anyone join me to eat?
I can't understand it; I haven't a hunch,
Why nobody sits with me when I eat lunch.

CHEWING USED GUM

I think that it is really neat
To find old gum beneath my seat.
I take a piece, chew and savor,
And try and guess its age and flavor.

With looks of disgust, the other kids stare
As I scrape a wad from beneath my chair.
I pop it in my mouth, chew and smile
Humming a tune all the while.

My taste buds have grown quite acute,
Is it grape, Big Red, or Juicy Fruit?
I'll tell you soon, for I've become
A connoisseur of used chewing gum.

WORM PIE

Here's a pie; it's made of mud
Plus several different kinds of crud.
It's organic, full of worms
And other kinds of yucky germs.

I got some dirt and mixed it up,
Then poured it in this paper cup.
I stirred it up, I added water,
And I'll sell it to you for a quarter!

HOLD THE FISH!

Double yuck! I don't believe ya.
You ordered anchovies on the pizza!
Sausage, onions, pepperoni's fine,
But no anchovies on the half that's mine.

They're really gross, those little fishes.
And you ordered them against my wishes!
Jeez, I really wish you'd grow up,
'cause just one bite would make me throw up.

I think you've got the grossest taste,
And it seems like such an awful waste.
Sometimes I think your senses leave ya,
When you order anchovies on the pizza!

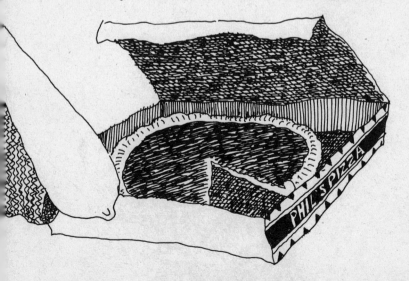

DON'T PICK YOUR NOSE

When dining out, I've got some tips:
Don't chew gum or smack your lips.
Picking your nose is considered rude.
Never stick your fingers in the food.

Keep your feet off the table,
Try not to burp, and, if you're able,
Don't fidget when you have to pee
But leave the table quietly.

If you follow these tips you'll be a winner
The next time you go out to dinner.
On second thought, it might be fitter,
If they left you home with a baby-sitter!

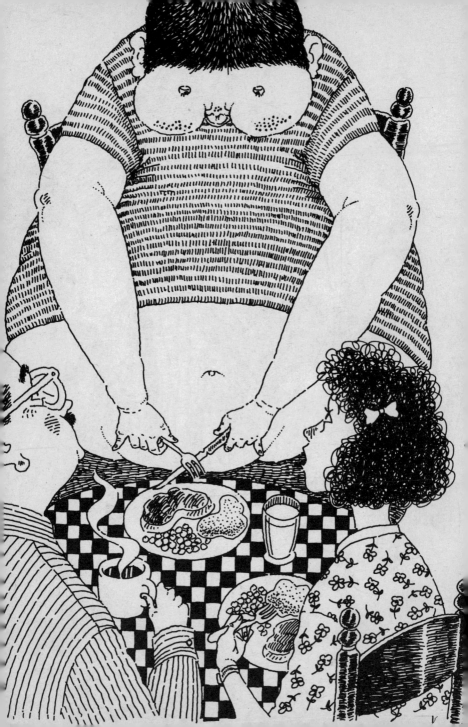

I'M NINE FEET TALL!

Dad looked at me
Quite seriously
The other night at dinner.
He said to Mom,
"I think that Tom
Is starting to get thinner!

"He didn't finish
His curried spinach.
And what's more, I fear,
If he doesn't eat
His rice and meat
He'll shrink and disappear!"

So I cleaned my plate,
And put on weight,
And grew up nine feet taller.
Mom said to Dad,
"I preferred the lad
When he was somewhat smaller!"

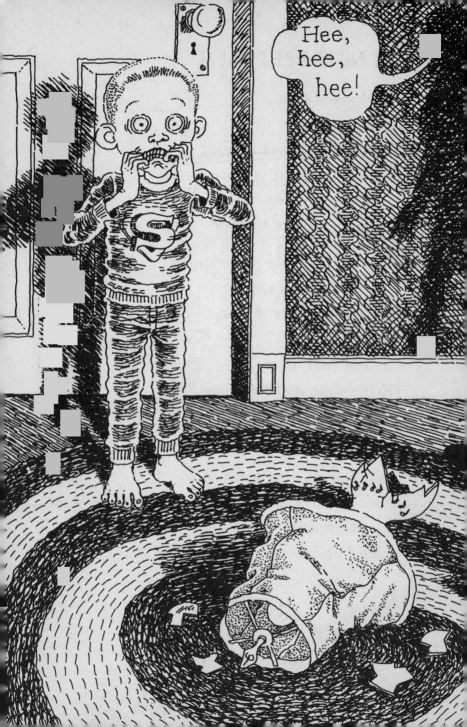

NOT ME!

Who locks you out, then loses the key,
When there's no one there for you to see?
Who leaves muddy footprints on the floor,
Breaks a dish, slams the door?

Who scratches the paint on the bedroom wall,
Or breaks the lamp in the upstairs hall?
Who spills the juice, who clogs the drain
When there's no one around but you to blame?

I know who. It really peeves me,
'cause Mom and Dad just won't believe me.
I didn't do it! Really! I swear!
It was the Invisible Man who isn't there!

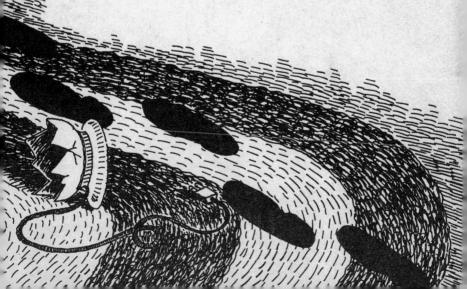

GOTCHA!

The monsters are coming! Oh no! Oh no!
I heard it on the radio.
The monsters are coming down the street,
I hear the *flip-flop* of their feet!

The monsters are coming up the walk.
I hear their snarling, nasty talk.
They gnash their teeth, pull their hair,
I hear them climbing up the stair!

The monsters are coming, they're at the door.
Sounds like there are fifty or more.
They knock and shout; they ring the bell,
They fill the air with horrid yells!

The monsters are coming, I'd better hide.
'cause pretty soon they'll be inside!
I guess I'll hide behind this chair,
They'll never think of looking there.

The monsters are coming, they're in the room!
Looking for me in the shadowy gloom!
The monsters are co—

ONLY CHILD

I wish bugs were crawling in your hair,
I wish your teeth were brown.
I wish you were kidnapped by a bear
That wandered into town!

If you disappeared into the wild,
I wouldn't even miss ya,
'cause then I'd be an only child
And you wouldn't be my sister!

MARY LOUISE

I had a kid sister named Mary Louise.
She wouldn't eat carrots, she wouldn't eat peas.
Mary Louise, Mary Louise,
Never said thank you, never said please.

My little sister, Mary Louise,
Liked to climb ladders, liked to climb trees.
Mary Louise, Mary Louise,
Had scabs on her elbows, scabs on her knees.

One day last December, Mary Louise
Caught a slight cold when exposed to the breeze.
Now I'm sad to report that Mary Louise
Exploded today when she stifled a sneeze.

BEN ON ICE

My brother, Ben, went out to play,
On the coldest winter's day.
Mom said, "Ben, wear your coat and hat."
But Ben went out, not doing that.

No coat, no hat, no scarf or sweater,
Ben was sure that he knew better.
What happened next was very squalid:
It seems that Ben got frozen solid!

Ben stood there frozen through the season,
Till spring thawed him out, and that's the reason,
Now when Ben goes out in any weather,
He *always* wears his coat and sweater!

IF A ZOMBIE ATE
MY MOM AND DAD

If a zombie ate my mom and dad,
I'd watch TV all day.
I wouldn't do my homework,
I'd just go out and play.

If a zombie ate my mom and dad,
I'd eat candy and drink Cokes,
Spend hours on the telephone
Telling knock-knock jokes.

If a zombie ate my mom and dad
There'd be no one to worry
Whether I got to bed on time,
Or telling me to hurry.

And though they make me clean my plate,
I guess I'm just as glad,
A zombie hasn't come around
To eat my mom and dad.

LOOK AT ME!

Look at me! Look at me!
I'm balancing six apples on my knee.
Juggling three pillows from my bed,
All this, while standing on my head!

Look at me! Look at me!
I'm really something! Look and see!
Now I'm twirling cups and a dinner plate.
Look at me! . . . Rats! Now it's too late.